The Shape of Home

RASHIN KHEIRIYEH

LQ

LEVINE QUERIDO

MONTCLAIR • AMSTERDAM • HOBOKEN

This is an Arthur A. Levine book

Published by Levine Querido

LQ

LEVINE QUERIDO

www.levinequerido.com · info@levinequerido.com

Levine Querido is distributed by Chronicle Books LLC

Text and illustrations copyright © 2021 by Rashin Kheiriyeh

Library of Congress Control Number: 2021932055

ISBN 978-1-64614-098-5

Printed and bound in Italy

Published in August 2021

First Printing

Book design by Patrick Collins

The text type was set in Adderville ITC Med.

The artwork for this book was created using oil and acrylic, watercolor, pencils, and pastels.
It includes collages that were created using papers that were colored and textured by hand.

*I dedicate this book
to every child with a wild imagination;
to those who see shapes in the clouds
that remind them of home.*

My name is Rashin, and today is my first day of school in America. I'm a little nervous about it.

My mom made breakfast shapes for fun: Look! A smiley-face pancake! A bear honey bottle! And happy eggs! See any others?

I hope my first day of school takes a great shape too!

I thought I would get to ride to school
with the other children on a lovely yellow
school bus, but it turns out I will walk!
My umbrella has the shape of a kitty!

When I was living in Iran, I would walk to school with my best friend, Azadeh. Every morning we would smell the fresh bread from Mr. Hassan's bakery. The shape of the bread was like my braided hair. Here they call it challah!

When I walk with my mom in New York City, everyone is in a rush—some people hurrying to work, some walking in the parks. I see them crossing the street in lines. I see circles on bikes and on car wheels.

Azadeh liked to collect the
blossoms under the orange tree, and
make necklaces and bracelets for us.
She made them in the shape of hearts.
They smelled so good.

We jumped over the small streams and
sometimes threw paper boats in the water and
raced them to school. They looked
like three triangles stuck together!

I was always the fastest girl, even though it was hard to run in our school uniforms. Guess what funny shape the uniforms gave us?

All the girls would wear long turquoise dresses with white hijabs around our heads.

When we walked to our school together, the boys at the school nearby would tease that we looked like a carton of eggs!

That made us laugh.

"Hi Rashin!" a girl from my neighborhood says
as I walk in the door.

"Oh, Aadiya! It is so awesome to see you here," I say.
We hug and sit next to each other.

I look around. The classroom is bright and happy. There are books everywhere but they all open backwards from books in Farsi, the language I spoke in Iran. And the letters have funny shapes too.

The teacher smiles at all of us.

"Hello class! My name is Mrs. Martin. I grew up in New Jersey, but my grandparents came from Benin, which is long and skinny—like me!"

That makes the class laugh.

"YOU are an exciting class because you come from so many different places. Why don't you all take a few minutes to think about it, and then we'll introduce ourselves and the place or places we come from."

CLASS B

Benin

"While you're thinking, I'll show you Benin. It's located in West Africa. The shape of my country looks a little like a flashlight. See what I mean? Where do your families come from?"

"My name is Akio, and my family came from Japan.
I think my country looks like a seahorse!" Akio says.
That makes me laugh.

Japan

Michael points out another
country on the map.
"My parents are from Italy,
but I was born here. Italy looks
like a boot." Michael shows
us his rain boots.

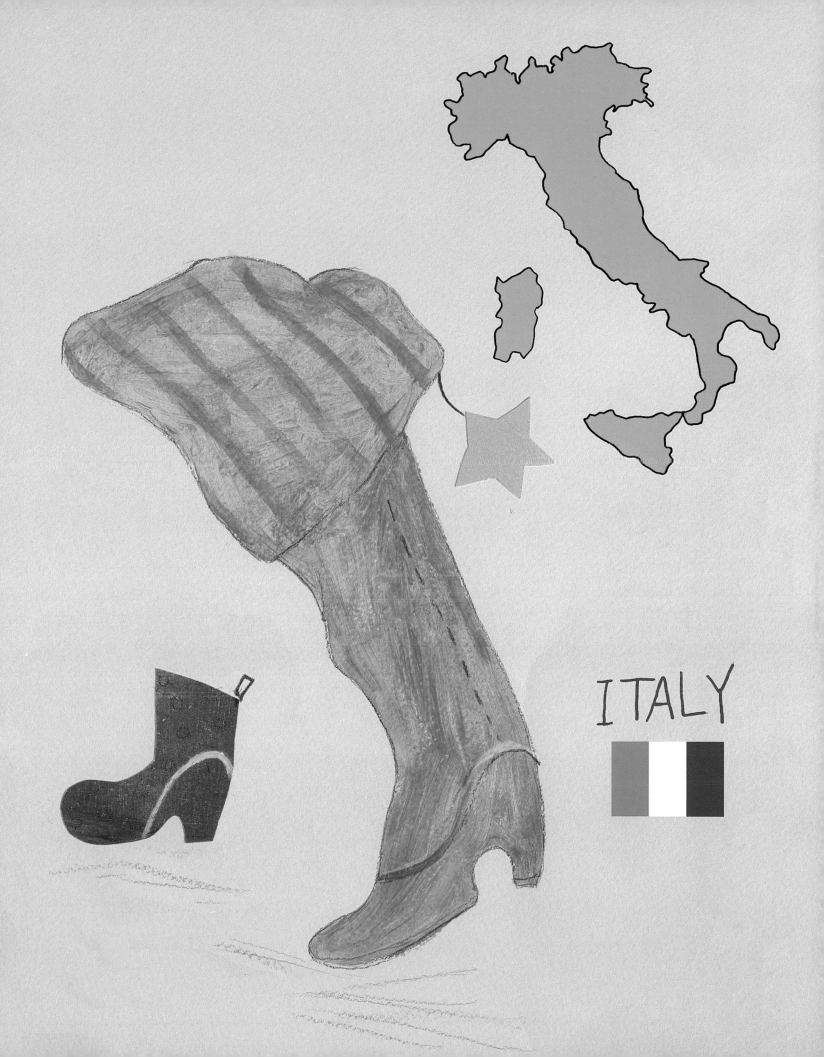

ITALY

"I am from India. My country looks like a
Hindu goddess," Aadiya says with a yoga pose.

INDIA

Now, it is my turn. I am so excited to introduce my country to the class!

"My name is Rashin, and I am from Iran. My country looks like a cat. A Persian cat, meow…"

I say this with a cat pose.

Everyone laughs, loud.

IRAN

When we are all done, Mrs. Martin asks us to imagine what various parts of the United States look like:

FLoRIDA

Aadiya says Florida looks like a dog's tongue.

I say Long Island looks like a fish swimming to the shore!

LONG ISLAND

Akio thinks New York looks like a big heart.

NEW YORK

Then we imagine a map of the
United States of America
using shapes. We think
it looks like this:

UNITED STATES OF AMERICA

And by the end of the day, my classroom is shaped like a home!